T.R. Bear

T.R.'s HALLOWE'EN

Terrance Dicks
Illustrated by Susan Hellard

YOUNG CORGI BOOKS

T.R. BEAR: T.R.'S HALLOWE'EN

A YOUNG CORGI BOOK 0 552 525073

Originally published in Great Britain in 1986 by Piccadilly Press Ltd.

PRINTING HISTORY
Piccadilly Press edition published 1986
Young Corgi edition published 1988

This book is set in 14/18 pt Century Book by Colset Private Limited, Singapore.

Young Corgi Books are published by Transworld Publishers Ltd., 61–63 Uxbridge Road, Ealing, London W5 5SA, in Australia by Transworld Publishers (Australia) Pty. Ltd., 15–23 Helles Avenue, Moorebank, NSW 2170, and in New Zealand by Transworld Publishers (N.Z.) Ltd., Cnr. Moselle and Waipareira Avenues, Henderson, Auckland.

Printed and bound in Great Britain by
The Guernsey Press Co. Ltd., Guernsey, Channel Islands.

Chapter One

A Great American Custom

'From ghoulies and ghosties,' chanted T.R. Bear, 'And long-leggety Beasties, And things that go BUMP in the night . . .'

Jimmy opened one eye and peered over the edge of the covers.

'What are you on about, T.R.?'

'Spooks!' said T.R. mysteriously. 'Witches and wizards and ghosts and goblins and ghouls! In a word, kid – Hallowe'en!'

'Hallo – what?' said a posh, tired-sounding voice.

This was Edward, Jimmy's other teddy bear.

'It's an American custom, Edward,' said a prim female voice.

This was Sally Ann, the rag doll, not Jimmy's really, but passed on to him by his big sister Jenny.

Sally Ann was a rather bossy doll, and seemed to know everything about everything.

Jimmy sat up in bed.

It was nice having toys that came to life and talked, but sometimes it got in the way of your sleep.

'Oh well, *American*,' said Edward wearily.

As an all-American bear, named after the famous President Theodore Roosevelt, T.R. was quick to defend his native land. 'Lissen, buster,' he began fiercely. 'Hallowe'en is a *great* American custom!'

Jimmy thought he'd better join in to stop an argument. 'It's all right, T.R., Edward's just being silly. Hallowe'en's an English custom too these days.'

'Well, I've never heard of it,' said Edward in an offended voice. 'What happens?'

'You all dress up,' explained Jimmy.

Edward sighed. 'What *as*?'

T.R. joined in. 'It's gotta be somethin' creepy, see? Ghosts, vampires, werewolves, that kinda stuff.'

'Ghosts are easiest,' said Jimmy. 'All you need is a white sheet!'

'Right,' said T.R. 'Devils are good too, but you need some kinda rubber mask.'

'I see,' said Edward, though it was quite clear he didn't. 'And when you're all dressed up in these spooky costumes, what do you do?'

'Trick or treat!' said Jimmy and T.R. both together.

'Trick or what?'

'It's quite simple,' explained Jimmy. 'You and your friends dress up in these spooky costumes, and then you go round the neighbourhood knocking on doors. When people answer, you say "Trick or treat!" '

'And what do they say?' Edward was still puzzled.

'Well, if they're nice, friendly people they give you some kind of treat – sweets mostly, or cakes or fruit, sometimes money.'

'Nearly right, kid,' said T.R. 'First you've gotta do some kinda good trick for them – tell a joke, sing a song, turn a somersault. That's the way we do it where I come from.'

'Good idea,' said Jimmy. 'We'll do it like that.'

'Steady on.' Edward sounded rather disapproving. 'What if they're not friendly? Suppose they don't want to see your trick? Suppose they tell you to clear off or don't even answer the door?'

T.R. rubbed his paws together. 'Then you give 'em the works!'

'What works?'

'You play the *other* kind of tricks on them. Sticky tape on the doorbell so it keeps on ringing. Lard on the doorknobs. Whitewash on the windows . . . Unwind a toilet roll all round the gate.' T.R. sounded as if he had a lot more tricks to describe, but Edward interrupted him.

'Why that's terrible!'

'Oh c'mon, don't be such a stuffed

shirt,' growled T.R. 'It's all done in fun!'

'Fun!' Edward Bear was outraged.

'Edward's got a point, you know, T.R.,' said Jimmy. 'We don't want to upset or frighten anyone.'

'Sure thing, kid,' said T.R. 'There's no way I'd play tricks on someone who'd be *really* scared.'

'Anyway,' said Jimmy. 'Most people just give you the treat, so you never get to play any tricks at all.'

'Too bad,' said T.R. 'Kinda takes all the fun out of it!'

Jimmy yawned. 'Why are you lot going on about Hallowe'en?'

'We're not,' said Sally Ann primly. 'T.R. is.'

'All right then,' said Jimmy. 'Why is T.R.?'

'Because it's this Sunday!' said T.R., excitedly. 'We gotta get organised!'

'All right,' said Jimmy sleepily, 'I'll see what I can do in the morning. Now, pipe down you lot and let me get some sleep!'

Jimmy flopped back down on his pillow and pulled the covers over his head.

As he drifted off to sleep he could hear the three toys chatting away on the toy shelf in low voices. 'You see, T.R.,' Sally Ann was saying, 'Hallowe'en is really a very ancient folk ceremony.'

Next day, which, luckily, was a Saturday, Jimmy started making plans for Hallowe'en.

The first thing he had to do was to

convince his mother that it was all right for them to go out trick or treating.

Every year his mother tried to persuade them not to go. Every year she finally agreed that it might just possibly be all right. 'But you're only to go up and down the street, to people we know. And you mustn't play any really nasty tricks on people even if they won't give you anything. And whatever you do, you mustn't disturb old Mrs Maltby.'

'Don't worry,' said Jimmy. 'Pretend witches for Hallowe'en are one thing, but I don't want to get mixed up with a real one!'

'That's very unkind, Jimmy. You know perfectly well old Mrs Maltby isn't really a witch. She's just a little – strange, that's all!'

Mrs Maltby lived in a big old-fashioned house at the bottom of Jimmy's street. The house stood a little apart from the others, set back from the road. It had a long winding driveway overhung with droopy bushes, and the house itself was tall and thin, with a crooked roof and twisted chimneys.

As if that wasn't enough, Mrs Maltby herself was tall and thin with a long, beaky nose and she strode up and down the street wrapped in a long black cloak and carrying a long cane.

Lots of the smaller kids in the street really believed that Mrs Maltby was a witch, and even some of the bigger ones weren't too sure she wasn't . . .

Jimmy and his brother and sister usually kept well away from Mrs Maltby at Hallowe'en.

But this year they didn't.

The results were absolutely horrendous.

And it was all T.R.'s fault . . .

Chapter Two

Trick or Treat

Next evening, just as it was getting dark, a mixed band of what T.R. might have called 'ghosties and ghoulies' was gathered in Jimmy's kitchen getting ready to set out.

There was Jenny, his older sister, wrapped in a black teacher's gown – borrowed from Jimmy's father who never used it – and wearing a home-made pointed hat. She'd even made herself a witch's broomstick from an ordinary broom handle and a bundle of twigs.

There was Jimmy's older brother George wearing their father's old black raincoat, slanting eyebrows and moustache, put on with make-up, and a set of fangs from the joke shop.

'Count Dracula to the life,' said Jimmy's mother admiringly. 'Or should I say, to the death?'

George smiled, and began practising his snarl.

Jimmy himself had settled for the standard ghost costume – an old sheet pulled over the head and gathered around the neck to make a

sort of hood. Eyeholes and a mouth-hole had been cut out of the head bit, with the holes outlined in thick black ink.

Then of course there was T.R.

As usual, he was tucked into Jimmy's school-bag with his head sticking out.

Only this time it wasn't T.R.'s usual furry head with the little round glasses. Instead it was the head of a demon, with horns, slanting eyes and fangs – and T.R.'s glasses perched on the demon's nose.

T.R.'s stubby teddy-bear body was wrapped in a red cloak made out of a bit of old curtain. He had insisted not only on coming but on dressing up as well, and the rubber demon-mask and red cloak had been the best Jimmy could manage.

Not that T.R. was complaining.

He was highly delighted with his new outfit. Up in Jimmy's bedroom when they were alone he had been strutting up and down in front of the mirror like the demon king in a pantomime. Now, of course, with other people about, he was sitting motionless, head sticking out of Jimmy's bag, pretending to be just an ordinary, non-talking toy bear.

But Jimmy knew differently, and he had a nasty feeling that once they got out there in the darkness, T.R. might easily get over-excited and out of control.

At first everything went well.

They worked their way up the street, calling at neighbours' houses and banging the knocker or ringing the bell.

When the neighbour came to the door, the terrifying trio jumped up and down, waving their arms, and cackling, 'Trick or treat! Trick or treat!' in spooky voices.

At this point the neighbour would sigh, say, 'Hello George, hello Jenny, hello Jimmy!' Some of them even added 'Hello, T.R.!' since it was well-known that Jimmy took T.R. with him almost everywhere.

Then Jimmy would do a hand-stand. Jenny would sing and George would tell some terrible old joke. (What's black and yellow and highly dangerous? Shark-infested custard!)

After that the neighbour would produce sweets, chocolate bars, apples, and the occasional 10p coin.

They only once got to play a trick, when crotchety old Mr Carney waved his stick at them and told them to 'Buzz off!' He did this every year, and every year they played a trick on him. (Jimmy always felt that secretly Mr Carney enjoyed it as much as they did.)

This year they jammed his bell-push with a match so the bell wouldn't stop ringing, and he came out again and chased them right down the street.

The next few neighbours paid up meekly, and Jimmy could sense that

T.R., sitting in his bag, was beginning to get bored.

They worked their way up one side of the street and down the other, and finally found themselves outside the gate of the big old house that belonged to Mrs Maltby, the old lady everyone said was a witch.

Jimmy was a little way ahead of the others, and suddenly he heard a deep, rumbling voice from the bag over his shoulder. 'Now, that's the kind of house to go and play trick or treat on!'

Jimmy looked up the winding drive to the crooked old house at the end, twisted chimneys outlined against the stormy sky. 'There? You're crazy, T.R. That's old Mrs Maltby's house. Everyone says she's a witch. Besides, look how spooky it looks down that drive.'

Unfortunately, T.R. wasn't discouraged. Just the reverse, in fact. 'That's the whole idea, kid. Hallowe'en is supposed to be spooky.'

The others caught up and George said, 'Having a nice chat to your teddy, Jimmy?' Stung by his tone, Jimmy said, 'I was just wondering if we should go and trick or treat Mrs Maltby?'

Jenny gave a gasp of horror. 'And risk getting turned into frogs for our trouble? I wouldn't dare!'

'Oh, she doesn't scare me, of course,' said George loftily.

'Well, you've got nothing to worry about, have you, George?' asked Jimmy innocently.

'What do you mean?'

Jimmy said, 'Well, if you got turned into a frog no one would ever know the difference!'

'I don't want any of your cheek,' said George angrily. 'You're only talking big because you know we won't let you go. If we agreed to go, you'd be off down the road like a shot, scuttling back home with your precious teddy-bear!'

Jimmy couldn't bear it when George talked to him like that. 'Oh, would I? We'll see!'

Before anyone could stop him, Jimmy unlatched the big iron gate that barred Mrs Maltby's driveway. It swung open with an eerie creaking sound.

Jimmy stepped onto the drive.

'Well, George,' he said challengingly. 'Coming?'

Defiantly, George followed him through the gate.

Then, of course, poor Jenny had to go too. As the sensible one, she felt she ought to try and keep the others out of trouble.

Both terrified, and both determined not to show it, George and Jimmy marched down the drive towards the old dark house. Jenny trailed worriedly behind.

'There doesn't seem to be any-one in,' said George nervously. 'Maybe we'd better just go home!'

Jimmy heard a mutinous rumbling from his school-bag and said hur-riedly, 'Oh no, you don't. We've got to bang on the door and ring the bell or it doesn't count.'

Bracing himself, Jimmy led the way forward.

He'd only gone a few steps when he realised he was on his own.

Jenny and George just weren't following.

'Come on,' he whispered.

George shook his head. 'I'm just not going.'

Jenny said, 'Sorry, Jimmy, but I'm not going either. Come on home.'

'When I've banged on the door and said trick or treat,' said Jimmy obstinately. 'I won't be long. You two can wait by the gate.'

From inside the bag a deep voice rumbled, 'Attaboy, kid!'

Encouraged by T.R.'s support, Jimmy marched on down the drive.

Shining the torch in front, Jimmy went up to the door. It was huge and studded with metal knobs, like the door to a castle – a witch's castle, thought Jimmy with a shudder.

To his secret relief, the house seemed to be in total darkness. Old Mrs Maltby must be out somewhere. With any luck he could bang on the door and then clear off without seeing her.

At least he'd be able to say he'd tried, and no one else had ever dared to do that before.

Reaching up, Jimmy banged the heavy metal knocker. It was made in the shape of a face and seemed to scowl warningly at him.

He gave three big bangs. One . . . two . . . three . . .

The sound boomed through the air and then faded away.

Jimmy remembered a poem they'd had to learn in school. Something about a traveller coming to a deserted house, knocking and getting no reply.

'Tell them I came and no one
answered.
Tell them I kept my word, he said.'
Something like that, anyway.

Suddenly Jimmy got his answer after all, though it wasn't the kind he was expecting.

A huge black shape swooshed out of the darkness behind him, and suddenly Mrs Maltby's bony hand was gripping his wrist, and her beaky-nosed face was peering into his own.

'Now I've got you!' she hissed. 'You won't get away now!'

Chapter Three

Accused!

For one awful moment Jimmy thought his worst nightmares were true, and Mrs Maltby really was a witch.

It was just as though she had swooped down from the night skies on her broomstick to catch him knocking, and ringing her door-bell.

Then he saw the angular metal

shape beside her and realised what had happened.

Mrs Maltby had arrived not by broomstick but by bike. The sound of the wind in the bushes must have covered the swishing of her tyres on the gravel, allowing her to arrive as if by magic.

But if she wasn't a witch she was still Mrs Maltby, and that was quite frightening enough.

'You don't understand,' said Jimmy desperately. 'It's only a game. We're doing trick or treat!'

'What?' she shrieked. 'What d'you say?'

Jimmy realised that she must be deaf as well as short-sighted.

Shouting at the top of his voice he tried to explain. 'Hallowe'en! Trick or treat . . . We knock on the door and you give us treats. If you don't we play tricks on you.'

'Treats? Tricks?'

Jimmy felt encouraged. 'Yes, sweets or money or something.'

'Money?' shrieked the old lady. 'You'll get no money from me, you little thief. I'll hand you over to the police!'

Realising that there was no chance of talking his way out of trouble, Jimmy gave a sudden determined heave and wrenched himself free.

As he turned to run, Mrs Maltby reached out to grab him again.

Luckily for Jimmy she was still holding her bicycle and couldn't move very fast. She did manage to catch hold of his school-bag for a moment, but Jimmy tugged hard, something gave and suddenly he was free.

Whirling round Jimmy dashed back down the drive and through the open front gate, ignoring the angry shrieks from behind him.

He found George and Jenny lurking worriedly just outside the front gate.

'What happened?' cried Jenny.

'Did she see you? We saw her turn into the drive but there was no way we could warn you!'

'She saw me all right,' said Jimmy. 'Grabbed me too. I managed to get away.'

'Do you think she recognised you?' asked George.

'I doubt it. You know the poor old thing's short-sighted as well as deaf.'

'You've had a lucky escape,' said George severely, just as if he hadn't been involved at all. 'I suggest we go straight home and all keep very quiet about all this. With any luck it'll all blow over.'

When they arrived back home, their mother was waiting in the big kitchen with the traditional cocoa and sandwiches.

'Did you have a good time?' she asked. 'How much did you get?'

'Get?' asked Jimmy.

His mother gave him a puzzled look. 'Tricking or treating. Or was it all tricks and no treats?'

Jimmy and the others began emptying their pockets of fruit, sweets and money.

'You've done very well,' said their mother. 'Though I must say you don't seem very pleased about it. Is something the matter? Was some-one nasty to you or something?'

For a moment Jimmy was tempted to confess everything, but then he thought that would mean getting the others in trouble too. Hurriedly, crossing his fingers behind his back, Jimmy said, 'No, no, everything's fine, Mum. Just a bit tired and hungry, that's all. Is the cocoa ready?'

His mother gave him a worried look, but she didn't say anything.

They all sat round eating and drinking in glum silence. It was very different from the usual Hallowe'en supper, thought Jimmy miserably.

'Look, there is something wrong, isn't there?' said their mother. 'Why don't you just tell me about it?'

Before anyone could answer the doorbell rang and they heard Dad calling, 'I'll go.'

The kitchen door opened and their father came in.

Behind him there was a policeman.

'This is Constable Parkin,' said their father grimly. 'I think he'd better tell you what he's here for himself.'

The policeman looked at the two boys. 'Which one of you is James?'

'Me,' said Jimmy.

The policeman looked sternly at him. 'We've had a complaint from an old lady who lives down the road, a Mrs Maltby.'

'All right,' said Jimmy wearily, 'I admit it. I should have owned up.'

The policeman looked even sterner. 'You admit it, do you?'

Jimmy turned to his mother. 'I'm sorry, Mum. I went to try and play trick or treat on Mrs Maltby. It was a sort of dare. She was out when I got there, but she turned up and caught me, and I ran away.'

His mother looked almost relieved.

'Is that all?' She looked reprovingly at Constable Parkin. 'Well, really! I'm sorry if Mrs Maltby was annoyed, and I'll see Jimmy goes round and says he's sorry, but I wouldn't have thought it was a matter for the police.'

'I'm afraid you don't understand, Madam,' said the policeman. 'Mrs Maltby tells a very different story. She says your son threatened her and demanded money.'

'She's got it all wrong,' said Jimmy desperately. 'I was trying to explain about trick or treat, how people sometimes give you sweets, or sometimes money. She wouldn't listen, so that's why I ran away.'

'You see?' said Jimmy's mother. 'It was just a misunderstanding. Mrs Maltby didn't realise it was all in fun. Jimmy's been very silly, but he hasn't done anything criminal.'

'That's a matter of opinion, Madam,' said the policeman. 'Mrs Maltby said that when she went back into the house after your son had run away, everything breakable in the front room had been broken, and apparently jewellery and ornaments are missing.'

He turned to Jimmy, holding

something up. 'Is this yours?'

He was holding the plastic luggage tag from Jimmy's bag. It was the kind that holds a little card so you can put your name and address on it.

Jimmy nodded. That was how the police had traced him so quickly.

'Yes, of course it's mine.' He nodded to the bag in the corner. 'It comes off that. She must have grabbed me by the tag and it came away when I broke free. Can I have it back?'

Carefully, the policeman put the tag back in his pocket. 'I'm afraid this is evidence, young man!'

Chapter Four

Sherlock Bear

For a moment there was a shocked silence.

Jimmy's dad said, 'What happens now?'

The policeman said, 'Mrs Maltby's coming down to the station tomorrow morning first thing, to sign a formal complaint. I suggest you all come down as well. I shall have to interview your son, and after that –' He shrugged. 'I'll be able to tell you if he is likely to end up in Juvenile Court.'

'I see. Well, thank you very much. We'll be down at the station tomorrow.'

They waited in silence while he showed the policeman out.

When his dad came back into the kitchen Jimmy said, 'I'm telling the truth, Dad. I did go up to the house, she caught me and I ran off. But I didn't damage anything and I didn't steal anything. I didn't even go into the house – and these two didn't get more than half way up the drive.'

'Don't worry, we believe you,' said

his father. 'I'm sure the police will as well.'

Their mother said, 'Do you think the old lady made the story up – just to get back at the children?'

'Maybe. I suggest you kids finish your sandwiches and get to bed.'

Jimmy didn't feel like eating any more, so he picked up his school-bag and went upstairs. Maybe T.R. would have an answer, he thought. At least they'd be able to talk it over once they were alone.

But when Jimmy sat down on his bed and opened his school-bag he got the third and biggest shock of the evening. T.R. wasn't there.

Jimmy sat still for a moment working out what had happened. He could half-remember zipping up the bag as he fled, so T.R. wouldn't fall out. By then he must already have fallen out – at the moment Mrs Maltby grabbed Jimmy's arm.

He hadn't actually seen T.R. at all after that, he realised.

Once he'd worked out what happened Jimmy knew what he had to do. He had to go back to Mrs Maltby's house and rescue T.R. Bear.

About ten minutes later Jimmy, wearing black jeans, a black sweater and a black raincoat, his face smeared with shoe-blacking and a pair of black wellies in his hand, was creeping ghost-like down the darkened stairs, school-bag over his shoulder. All this commando stuff seemed a bit much, but he couldn't see any other way. Pointless asking his parents to let him go for T.R., they'd never agree.

He crept silently past the half-open kitchen door, and heard his parents talking in low, worried voices.

They didn't hear him, but Harbottle, the big shapeless family dog did and came woofling out, tail wagging, hoping for a late-night walk.

'Get off, you great fool, you can't come,' whispered Jimmy. Then he thought, why not? It would be very dark and spooky going back to the old house, and even Harbottle would be some company.

Grabbing Harbottle by the collar Jimmy dragged him out of the front door, closing it very quietly behind him.

It didn't take long to reach the old dark house, and Jimmy looked up the long drive, bracing himself for the trip.

The drive looked longer and

spookier than ever, and the big old house at the end looked like Dracula's castle.

There was a light on in the front room of the house and Jimmy realised he'd have to go right up to the porch to start looking for T.R.

He crept along as silently as he could right up on to the front porch, took his torch out of the bag and shone it round. T.R. was nowhere to be seen.

Suddenly he saw a crumpled red scrap of cloth. T.R.'s cloak. Jimmy gave a low groan. He'd been thinking about T.R. as if the little bear were an ordinary toy, powerless to move. But T.R. could come to life when he wanted to and he was quite capable of just getting up and walking off.

Suddenly a voice hissed, 'Hey, kid, down here!'

Jimmy turned and saw a demon peering up at him.

He jumped back, then realised it was T.R. still in his devil mask. Harbottle whined a welcome. T.R. tugged at the mask. 'Help me get this thing off, willya, kid?' whispered T.R.

Jimmy took off T.R.'s glasses,

helped him to pull off the mask and then put the glasses back on.

T.R. heaved a sigh of relief. 'Thanks. Boy, it was hot in that thing!'

'Come on,' said Jimmy, 'we'd better get home.'

'Are you crazy?' said T.R. 'We gotta job to do here.'

'What do you mean? I'm in a lot of trouble as it is, T.R. I just want to get home before I make things any worse.'

'Take it easy,' rumbled T.R. 'Just tell me what happened.'

Jimmy told him the whole story and when he'd finished T.R. said, 'Right, now I get the picture.'

'I wish I did! Go on, Sherlock Bear, tell me about it!'

'Then listen. While you were on your way here to do your trick or treat there was a real live burglary going on here. Two of them, one fat one thin, just like Laurel and Hardy. You guys come up the lane flashing your torch and they think you're the cops and beat it. The old lady comes home, chases you off, goes back in the house, finds the mess left by the burglary and fingers you for the caper! You've been framed, kid.'

'Then how do I get out?'

'By helping me catch the bad guys!'

'How? They'll be miles away by now.'

'Nope,' said T.R. 'You see, they weren't sure you were the cops so they didn't beat it very far. Just into those bushes on the other side of the garden.'

'How do you know?'

'Because I saw them come out – about five minutes ago.'

'Which way did they go?'

T.R. jerked a thumb towards the house. 'Thataway!'

'What?'

'That's right, kid. They're back in the house. Finishing the burglary you interrupted.'

'What about the old lady?'

'She's still in the house too,' said T.R. 'And we gotta do something about it – right now!'

Chapter Five

T.R. to the Rescue

Jimmy wasn't too keen on taking on two thugs with the help of a teddy bear and a particularly soppy dog.

But as T.R. was always saying, 'A bear's gotta do what a bear's gotta do,' and the same was true of boys.

Jimmy sighed. 'Okay, T.R. What do we do?'

'We check out our resources, kid. Then we make a plan.'

'What resources? What plan?'

'To begin with, what have you got in that school-bag? Any weapons? A Colt .45 would come in handy.'

Jimmy began to rummage. 'Well, all I've got is a catapult; a torch and a few bangers.'

'Bangers?'

'Fireworks. Those little ones in a tube that go off really loud.'

Jimmy fished out the catapult and T.R. looked at it in disgust.

'Not much in the way of artillery. Can you shoot that thing?'

'I'm pretty good with it, actually,' said Jimmy modestly.

'You better be! Okay, kid, now listen good. Here's my plan . . .'

A few minutes later Jimmy and T.R. were creeping into the house, leaving a nervous Harbottle on guard outside.

The door was still ajar, so they got inside without trouble.

As they crept down the gloomy hall, they heard voices coming from the front room.

'They're in there,' whispered T.R. 'Gimme the fireworks and matches, kid, and be standing by!'

There was just one small lamp burning in the front room, which seemed to be crowded with pictures, ornaments and stuffed animals, many of them broken. The lamp stood on a small table beside a big armchair, and in the armchair sat Mrs Maltby with two men, one fat and one thin, standing over her.

On the floor nearby was a tele phone with the hand-piece knocked away from the stand.

'Listen, lady,' the fat man was saying. 'Just tell us where the money is and we'll go and you won't get hurt.'

Mrs Maltby glared back at him unafraid. 'Don't be so stupid. There is no money.'

'Come off it,' growled the thin man. 'Everyone knows you keep a big pile of banknotes hidden in the house.'

'Oh they do, do they?' Mrs Maltby seemed amused. 'You poor man, that's just silly gossip. My husband left me this house and everything in it when he died. Old-fashioned furniture, old-fashioned pictures and ornaments, hideous, most of them. But that's all I have. Apart from my old age pension there's no money at all!'

'Don't give me that,' snarled the fat man. 'Now give us the money or you'll be sorry.' And he raised his hand threateningly.

T.R. tapped Jimmy on the leg and pointed to a big green vase on the mantelpiece just behind the two burglars. 'Okay, kid?'

Jimmy had collected some pieces of gravel from the path, big chunky ones. He fitted one in his catapult and nodded.

Suddenly T.R. gave out a deep angry bellow. 'Okay, this is the cops. Everybody freeze!'

In the same moment he lit a banger and threw it into the corner of the room, aiming it well away from Mrs Maltby and the two men.

Jimmy took aim with his catapult and fired.

The banger went off with a tremendous BOOM!

At the same moment, the green vase exploded into a thousand fragments.

It looked exactly as if someone had shot the vase off the mantelpiece with a huge revolver.

'That was just a warning shot,' boomed T.R. 'The next guy that moves gets blasted!'

The two burglars stood like statues.

'Hands up,' ordered T.R. 'Turn round and face the fireplace!'

Hands in the air, the two men turned round.

'Reckon you could reach that phone, Ma'am?' called T.R.

'I most certainly could,' said Mrs Maltby. She struggled up, snatched up the phone and dialled 999. When the operator came on the line she gave her name and address and added, 'We've just captured two burglars for you. Kindly come and collect them!'

'Well done, sir,' called Mrs Maltby. 'I'm very grateful to you.'

'Heck, it was nothing, Ma'am,' said T.R. bashfully.

'You're American, aren't you?'

'I sure am, Ma'am.'

'May I ask your name?' Mrs Maltby peered into the darkness by the door.

They heard the sound of a police car's siren.

'No need for names, Ma'am,' said T.R. hurriedly. 'Just a passing stranger, glad to help. But there is something you could do for me.'

'Anything at all, my dear man.'

'I hear some kid got accused of wrecking your place and stealing, while it was these guys here all along. You might make sure the police get the right story this time.'

'I will, I promise!'

There was the sound of tyres on the gravel and the lights of a police car shone through the window.

Jimmy and T.R. slipped back into the darkened hallway as two large policemen pounded past them into the front room.

Slipping through the open door, Jimmy and T.R. disappeared into the night, Harbottle lolloping happily behind them.

Next morning Jimmy's mother woke him from a deep sleep. 'Wake up, Jimmy, wake up! Wonderful news!'

Jimmy yawned and stretched. 'All right, all right . . . Wassermatter?'

'That policeman came round again last night while you were in bed. He said a police car caught two burglars at Mrs Maltby's house last night. They did all the stealing and the damage, and the police are quite sure that you're innocent!'

Jimmy yawned again. 'Jolly good.'

'You don't seem very surprised!' said his father.

'Well, I knew I didn't do it all along,' pointed out Jimmy. 'Still, I'm glad it's been cleared up.'

'I wouldn't say that,' said his mother. 'Apparently, Mrs Maltby swears some mysterious American turned up, captured the burglars and held them prisoner at gunpoint and then just disappeared when the police arrived. He wouldn't even give his name.'

'It must have been the Lone Ranger,' said Jimmy's dad.

Jimmy looked up at the shelf where T.R. sat with the other toys and grinned.

As his parents went downstairs Jimmy said softly, 'Say, who was that mysterious masked bear?'

And from the toy shelf there came a faint, triumphant whisper. 'Hi-ho, Silver, awaaay . . .'

THE END